The Magic Secrets Box

The Silver City Ballet

To Elissa Brothwell
with lots of love
~ SM

With special thanks to ML
~ AD

STRIPES PUBLISHING
An imprint of Magi Publications
1 The Coda Centre, 189 Munster Road,
London SW6 6AW

A paperback original
First published in Great Britain in 2011

Text copyright © Sue Mongredien, 2011
Illustrations copyright © Artful Doodlers, 2011
Music supplied under licence & copyright © N J Dean & Co, 2011

ISBN: 978-1-84715-184-1

A CIP catalogue record for this book is available
from the British Library.

Printed and bound in China.

STP/1800/0005/0511

2 4 6 8 10 9 7 5 3 1

The Magic Secrets Box

The
Silver City Ballet

SUE MONGREDIEN

Stripes

Misty Mountains

White Frost

Evergreen Forest

Golden
Spires

The Magic Secrets Box

Prologue

The spell-chamber was cold and shadowy, with just the sound of the old enchanter's breathing to disturb the silence. Sorcero polished his magic magnifying glass, then held it over a large map spread out on the table. The map showed the Land of Eight Kingdoms, and as he moved the glass over Silver City and the Misty Mountains, tiny flickering images appeared on its surface, showing the enchanter what was happening there.

He grunted as he saw rainbow birds soaring in the kingdom of the Azure Skies, and snow-foxes hunting in the kingdom of White Frost. He scowled as he saw a troll lumbering through the Evergreen Forest. *Where was she?*

Sorcero hunched over the map, drawing his thick black cloak closer. He had to find her. He had to know what she was doing.

He moved the magnifying glass over the kingdom of Sunny Meadows and an image appeared of a group of young fairies flying after a smiling figure. Sorcero stiffened. There she was – the Fairy Queen, her wings shimmering, a small golden crown atop her chestnut hair. "Got you," he snarled.

He glowered as she waved her wand and a stream of butterflies billowed from it. The fairies clapped and cheered.

Once, Sorcero had been the one to delight the young fairies, elves, mermaids and children throughout the land. Not any more though. Not since he'd grown old and the Kings and Queens of the land had

retired him, and given the role to the Fairy Queen instead.

At first Sorcero had felt saddened by this; he missed the youngsters. But as time went by, where his heart had once been full of goodness and kindness, an iciness took hold and began to harden. Now he no longer felt sad. He felt angry that he'd been cast aside, and he wanted to punish the Fairy Queen for taking his place.

He'd find a way to stop her, he vowed. And when she was out of the way, he'd make everyone see that he, Sorcero, should never have been replaced.

He reached for his wand and pointed it at the Fairy Queen. Without taking his eyes off her, he began to recite a powerful spell. Then there was a puff of foul-smelling black smoke and the enchanter vanished.

The Magic Secrets Box

Chapter One

*M*egan Andrews trailed along the busy street behind her parents, glad it was time to go home. She was fed up with shopping! They'd had to wait ages to get her feet measured for new school shoes, and then even longer getting her school uniform. Megan was bored and hungry, and every time she saw the bags of school clothes swinging from the handles of her brother Liam's buggy, she felt sick at the thought of having to wear them on Monday. She wished the summer holidays didn't have to end.

They were walking back to the car park now, along a quiet alleyway that had cobbled paving and old-fashioned lamp posts. There were a few shops with tired-looking signs – a watchmaker's shop, an old-fashioned barber's, and what looked like a second-hand shop.

Megan's dad peered through the window. "Grandma and Grandpa used to have a chair just like that," he told Megan, pointing at an armchair that had curved wooden arms and a faded green velvet seat. "Grandpa dozed off in it every evening after work."

Megan smiled. Then something else in the window caught her eye – a small, colourful box with its lid up. She stepped closer and gazed in, shielding her eyes with her hand so that she could see better.

The box had little pictures on its surface, painted in pink, purple and blue. Inside, it was lined with a pale pink fabric, and there was a gleaming heart-shaped mirror in the lid. A dainty fairy figure was standing in front of it. She was wearing a white dress and gauzy silver-tipped wings, and held a tiny wand.

As Megan's eyes fell on the fairy figure, she had the strangest feeling that there was something special about her. And as her gaze lingered, the tiny fairy seemed to be staring right back at her, with a pleading expression on her face.

Megan blinked and looked away. She was being silly, wasn't she? "Too much imagination for her own good!" as Mrs Grey had said on her school report last year. "If Megan could stop daydreaming, she could do so much better…"

"Megan, are you even listening?" came her mum's voice suddenly. "You're away with the fairies again!"

Megan whirled round guiltily.

"I was just saying, shall we go?" Mrs Andrews repeated, looking bemused.

Megan glanced back at the shop window

and hesitated. For some reason, she didn't want to walk away from the fairy. "Um... Can I just see how much this box costs?" she found herself saying. "I've got four pounds left of my birthday money."

Her mum nodded. "The little music box? It's sweet, isn't it? I used to have one a bit like that. There's probably a key at the back – if you wind it up, the ballerina will spin round and music will play."

"It's not a ballerina, it's a fairy," Megan said, already walking into the shop. Her dad followed her inside, but Liam let out a wail of anguish at the prospect of more shopping.

"I'll take Liam to the car," Megan heard her mum say. "I'll see you two back there in a few minutes."

Inside, the shop smelled rather musty,

as if everything had been untouched for hundreds of years. A man was behind the counter, polishing a brass coal-scuttle. He looked up as the bell on the door jangled. "Hello!" he said, sounding rather surprised to see customers. "How can I help?"

"I just wanted to know how much the box in the window costs, please," Megan replied. "The one with the fairy in it?"

The man put down the cleaning rag and wiped his hands on his apron. "The box with the fairy in it?" he repeated, a small frown creasing his forehead. "I don't… Oh," he said, as Megan pointed to it. He reached into the window display and picked it up. "How funny, I don't remember this coming into the shop at all. My assistant must have put it there. Let's see if it works."

He turned the golden key at the back of the box once, twice, three times. There was a mechanical clicking sound … but nothing happened. "Ahh," he said. "I'm afraid it seems to be broken."

"Never mind, Meg," Dad said, making as if to leave the shop.

"Wait," Megan said. She had that strange feeling inside again. "I still want to buy it. I don't mind that it's broken."

"Are you sure?" Dad asked. "Wouldn't you rather have a new one that works?"

Megan shook her head. She wasn't sure why, but she just knew she had to buy the box. "I don't mind," she said again.

"Well, it's yours for a pound," the shopkeeper said.

"Thank you," Megan said, taking a coin from her purse. She could see the fairy figure's face better now, and of course it was completely still, the eyes staring straight ahead, the mouth held in a fixed painted smile. She shook herself. Fancy imagining that the fairy was looking at her!

Mrs Grey was right. Sometimes her imagination made her think silly things.

As soon as they got home, Megan raced upstairs to her room, clutching the music box. She put it on her bed, lifted the lid and wound the key at the back, just to double-check it wasn't working. The key made a clicking noise as it turned … and then, to Megan's surprise, tinkling music began to play and the fairy figure spun, rather stiffly at first, and then more smoothly.

Megan beamed. It *did* work!

But then something strange happened. Over the sound of the tinkling music, she heard a tiny voice. "Help!" called the voice. "Help me!"

The Magic Secrets Box

Chapter Two

*M*egan blinked in surprise. Where had the voice come from? Had she imagined it?

Then it came again. "Help! Help me!"

This time, the music had just died away with a last click, so the tiny voice was very clear. Megan hadn't imagined it. She jumped to her feet, her heart pounding, and gazed around the room. "W-who said that?" she stammered.

"I did," came the tiny voice.

Megan looked back down at the music box and her eyes nearly popped out of

her head. The fairy figure's mouth was moving! "Hello," she said. "Will you help me?"

Megan stared at the fairy's anxious face. "Are you in my imagination?" she whispered. "How come you can talk?"

The fairy smiled. "You can hear me – that's wonderful!" she cried. "I've been hoping and hoping a little girl would come along and take this box home. When I saw you look through the shop window at me today, I just knew you would help me."

"Help you do what? I don't understand," Megan said nervously. "Are you … are you magic?"

"Yes," the fairy said proudly. "I'm the Fairy Queen from the Land of Eight Kingdoms. I use my magic to fulfil good

deeds throughout the land, and look after all the youngsters. Well, I used to … until Sorcero captured me and trapped me inside this box."

"Sorcero?" Megan repeated. "Who's he?"

The fairy sighed. "He's an old magician," she replied. "He used to be a good, kind enchanter – in fact, he did my job before me. But he became jealous and angry when I was asked to replace him after he retired, and now his heart has turned quite cold. It is he who has trapped me here. And now I can't move anything but my eyes and mouth. I am a prisoner!"

Megan bit her lip. "Can I do something to help?" she asked. "Surely you don't have to stay in this box for ever?"

"I hope not," the fairy said. "The good news is, I think there is still some magic in my wand. It has been giving out little silver sparkles every now and then, although they're not as powerful as usual. I can feel some magic within this box too, even though I can't control it myself. I have no feeling in my hands to move my wand, but I have been wondering if perhaps another person might be able to use its magic by touching it."

Megan's eyes widened. "You mean … another person like me?" she asked, feeling goosebumps prickle up her arms.

"I hope so," the fairy replied. "Perhaps if you touch the wand, and I wish very hard, then some magic may happen. Shall we give it a try?"

Megan could hardly believe what the fairy was saying to her, but she so wanted to help. "Y-y-yes, please," she stammered.

She reached over to touch the end of the tiny wand, then the Fairy Queen commanded, "Show Megan how Sorcero trapped me here!"

Megan gasped as the tip of the wand seemed to pulse between her fingers and a stream of silver sparkles tumbled out, glittering round the edge of the heart-shaped mirror in the lid of the box. And then, to her amazement, an image appeared inside the mirror … an image of a flowery meadow, full of laughing young fairies and a pretty, smiling Fairy Queen…

"That's you!" Megan said, transfixed.

"Keep watching," said the Fairy Queen.

Megan could hear faint sounds from the scene in the mirror: the fairies' high voices and birds calling to one another. Then the little fairies vanished and a figure in a hooded cloak appeared. He had a long grey beard and a craggy, cold face. He raised his wand and pointed it at the Fairy Queen.

"Sorcero!" she gasped. "What are you—"

"You took my job from me," he sneered, "so I'm here to take something from you."

He swished the wand through the air, muttering evil-sounding enchantments under his breath. Then he let out a cry of laughter as black and purple plumes of smoke swirled out of his wand, wreathing themselves round the Fairy Queen.

"No! Please, stop!" She gasped and coughed, and tried to push the smoke away, but it clung fast to her. As it did so, a silver shimmering light appeared around her body and was quickly engulfed by the smoke. The smoke and silver light crackled together as if they were charged with electricity, then Sorcero shouted a command, and the silver light poured into his wand. His wild laughter echoed round the meadow as the last of the light disappeared.

Back in her bedroom, Megan felt a shiver go through her. "What did he do to you?" she asked in a whisper.

The painted face of the Fairy Queen in the music box looked sad. "He stole almost every drop of my magic."

In the mirror, Megan could see the old magician pointing his wand at the Fairy Queen again, a spiteful smile twisting his mouth. "And now to make you completely useless, just as you made me when you took my job," he snarled. "I'll change you into a doll, a powerless figurine, to spend the rest of your life in a child's music box." He waved his wand and more of the smoke belched out, enveloping the Fairy Queen and making her shrink until she was the size of a small doll.

Sorcero picked up the tiny Fairy Queen and examined her stiff, unmoving figure. "Perfect!" he laughed.

The Fairy Queen looked furious. "You can't do this!" she raged at him. "My magic is needed throughout the Eight Kingdoms! They need me, you've got to set me free!"

"Everyone will have forgotten about you by tomorrow," he gloated. "And I'll be there instead. Nice Sorcero. Kind Sorcero. All that's left to do now is to send you into the human world for ever!"

He raised his wand again, but the tiny fairy figure in his hand let out a cry. "Wait. Please! Is there any way this enchantment can be broken?"

Sorcero chuckled. "Only a true friend of all the Eight Kingdoms can set you free. Ha! Unfortunately for you, nobody in the human world will be able to do that. Say goodbye to Sunny Meadows, little fairy. You won't be back here ever again!"

And as he muttered another spell, the image in the music-box mirror faded and disappeared.

The Magic Secrets Box

Chapter Three

*M*egan blinked as her own reflection stared back at her in the mirror. "W-wow," she stuttered. "That was scary."

"It was," the Fairy Queen agreed. "But I have been thinking of what Sorcero said – about how only a true friend of the Eight Kingdoms could set me free. I'm wondering if you might be that friend."

"Me?" Megan said. "But I've never even heard of the Eight Kingdoms."

Before the Fairy Queen could reply, Megan's bedroom door opened and her mum appeared.

"Who are you talking to in here?" she asked, smiling. "Are you playing a game?"

Megan blushed furiously. "Um … yeah," she said, crossing her fingers behind her back. "Just playing with…" She glanced around quickly, her eyes falling on the collection of teddy bears on her bed, "…my bears."

"OK, well, it'll be lunch time in five minutes," her mum said. "So finish your game and wash your hands before you come down, all right?"

Megan nodded. She waited until her mum had closed the door and she heard footsteps moving away, then turned anxiously back to the Fairy Queen, her heart racing. She hoped the magic hadn't stopped! "Are you still there?" she whispered.

"Yes," the Fairy Queen replied. "The Land of Eight Kingdoms is not of your world," she explained. "It is a land in the fairy realm, founded by eight friends, whose descendants rule each kingdom to this day. I know that human kindness is a powerful thing. Perhaps if you were to visit each kingdom and be a friend to the person who needs it the most there, your kindness and friendship may be enough to break Sorcero's enchantment."

"Right," said Megan uncertainly.

"I need you to find out what Sorcero is doing, too," the Fairy Queen went on. "I'm worried that he is up to no good. Do you think you can help me? You must promise to keep this a secret! If Sorcero were to find out that you were helping me, he might turn his bad magic on you."

Megan gulped. Having seen Sorcero for herself in the mirror, she certainly didn't want that to happen. But she did want to help the Fairy Queen. "I'll try," she said. "How do I get to the Land of Eight Kingdoms? I still don't really understand."

The Fairy Queen's painted lips turned upwards in a smile. "Touch the tip of my wand," she instructed.

Megan hesitated. Hadn't Mum just said lunch was almost ready? "Am I going now?" she asked. "But what will I say to my mum and dad? They'll be worried about me – I can't just disappear."

"No one needs to know you've gone," the Fairy Queen assured her. "Any adventures in the Eight Kingdoms will seem like a split second in the human world." She smiled. "I promise you won't miss your lunch."

Megan thought for a moment. Her mind felt as if someone had tipped it upside down and given it a good shake. She was still half expecting to wake up at any moment and discover that the whole

thing had been a weird dream.

She took a deep breath. "OK," she said. "Here goes." She reached out and touched the tip of the Fairy Queen's wand, holding it between her finger and thumb.

The Fairy Queen smiled encouragingly. "Very good," she said. "Now you need to say 'Let me be a friend to the person who needs me most.'"

Feeling slightly self-conscious, Megan whispered, "Let me be a friend to the person who needs me most."

In the very next second, she heard the tinkling music again, ringing in her ears. A stream of silver sparkles tumbled from the wand, then her bedroom vanished from sight.

Megan couldn't see anything. The whole world seemed to have completely disappeared. She felt as if she was being pulled very fast through the air, with bright lights flashing like fireworks before her eyes. She could feel nothing beneath her arms and legs but cold empty air.

She was just starting to panic when she felt herself slowing down and coming to a stop. Her feet landed on the ground, and the world swung into focus.

She stared around curiously. She was on a street that looked quite normal at first glance, but then she noticed that actually everything was slightly different

from her world. The pavements and buildings had a silvery gleam to them. There was no traffic at all. Trees grew at intervals along the street, but they were like no other trees she'd ever seen before. These had long jaggedy leaves coloured a dark green with silver veins running through them like glittering thread.

There were holes in some of the buildings nearby – windows had been smashed, and bricks had crumbled away. Was this something to do with Sorcero's magic? He hadn't said exactly what he planned to do while the Fairy Queen was out of the way, but Megan had seen for herself just how nasty he could be.

She glanced around, suddenly nervous that he might appear round the corner and use some of his horrible magic smoke on her. She was supposed to be helping somebody, she remembered, but who?

A breeze ruffled the leaves of the trees and they made a gentle tinkling sound as they moved. Megan shivered and realized she was no longer wearing the jeans and top she'd been in a minute ago. Instead, she was dressed in a pale pink leotard, a full net skirt, white tights and pink satin ballet slippers tied with criss-cross ribbons round her ankles. She patted her hair and was surprised to find it was coiled in a neat bun on top of her head. *Whoa.* Fairy magic was cool! Was her outfit a clue, perhaps, to the person she had to help?

Just then, a window opened in the building above her and a stern-faced woman leaned out. Her hair was swept up in a bun just like Megan's. "Come on," she called. "Class is about to start. Hurry!"

The window shut again and Megan felt more confused than ever. But then she saw a sign by the door of the building: *Eliza Swann's Ballet Academy.* "I guess that's where I'm supposed to go," she said to herself. And she walked up the front steps and through the door.

Chapter Four

Megan had taken ballet classes for two years, but then she'd dropped ballet in favour of drama club. It felt strange walking into the academy now and seeing a group of other girls in matching pink leotards and ballet shoes waiting to go into their class. They were all chattering, their heads bent close together, except for one girl who stood apart from the others, looking rather unhappy.

The Fairy Queen's words about being a friend to the person who needed one

most rang in Megan's ears. She still wasn't completely convinced that being friendly to someone in this strange place could help the Fairy Queen return to her world, but she walked up to the girl nonetheless. "Hi, I'm Megan," she said with a smile.

"I'm Jessica," the girl replied. She had the most amazing silvery eyes, although right now they looked anxious. "I'm new to Silver City," she added shyly. "I've only been at the academy for a few weeks, and the other girls all seem to be best friends."

Silver City! thought Megan. *So that's where I am.* "Well, this is my very first day here," she replied truthfully. "And I don't know anyone in the class either. Maybe we could be partners?"

Jessica's cheeks turned pink. "I'd like that," she said with a small smile.

"Good," said Megan. Then she remembered the Fairy Queen's request to try to find out what Sorcero was up to. "Hey, do you know what's happened to all the buildings?" she asked casually. "They look as if they're about to fall down."

Jessica seemed surprised at Megan's question. "Do you mean the damage the giant's done to them?" she asked.

"Giant?" echoed Megan in alarm.

"Yes, the giant," Jessica said. "Haven't you heard? An evil giant from the Misty Mountains has been coming down to the city and smashing everything in sight. If you see him, run for your life."

"Oh, *that* giant," said Megan quickly. "Of course." *Perhaps this has something to do with Sorcero*, she thought. Maybe he'd commanded the giant to damage the buildings as part of some evil plan?

Before she could ask Jessica anything else, the stern-looking woman with a bun appeared. She was dressed in a black leotard and footless tights. The girls immediately stopped chattering and dipped their knees in little curtseys.

"Good morning, Madame Swann," they chorused in low voices.

Megan hastily curtseyed too.

Madame Swann led the girls up a flight of stairs, then unlocked a door. "Come," she said, ushering them inside.

Megan's legs felt trembly as she followed Jessica and the other dancers into the studio. There was an enormous mirror along one wall, and a wooden barre running in front of it. The wall opposite the mirror was almost all glass, giving an incredible view over Silver City.

The buildings stretched as far as the eye could see, their rooftops gleaming silver in the sunlight. The Land of Eight Kingdoms was really cool!

"Class, I have bad news," said Madame Swann, once everyone was at the barre. "Our royal performance at the Silver City theatre tonight has had to be cancelled."

A cry of dismay rang round the studio.

"Unfortunately, that wicked giant was blundering about in the dark last night," Madame Swann went on. "He walked straight into the theatre and knocked the roof clean off."

Jessica's face fell. "Oh no," she sighed. "I was so looking forward to dancing in front of the King and Queen."

The other girls looked disappointed, too. "Maybe we can do the show

somewhere else?" suggested a tall girl with jet-black hair and rather pointy elf-like ears.

"I'm afraid not," Madame Swann replied. "There's nowhere else in Silver City big enough for our audience and grand enough for our royal guests." She put her hands on her hips. "But come, let us dance away our disappointment. Begin your warm-up, please, girls, and then we will start today's lesson."

Around the room, each girl took hold of the barre and began performing a series of exercises. *Help*, Megan thought to herself, trying her best to copy Jessica's movements. *Any minute now Madame Swann is going to notice that I don't know the steps, and she'll realize I'm an impostor. I'll be thrown out of the class – and what will I do then?*

Chapter Five

Just as Madame Swann's eyes were beginning to narrow suspiciously at Megan as she went through the exercises, she – and everyone else – was distracted by a thunderous sound from outside the building. The floor of the studio began to shake and the girls all looked at each other in fear. What was happening? *Is it an earthquake?* Megan wondered, as she clutched the barre to steady herself.

Then they saw a pair of enormous legs striding past the window. "It's the giant!" one of the girls screamed.

Everybody gasped as the giant sank into a kneeling position on the road outside, and an enormous head appeared at the window. The giant peered into the room, staring at them, as if he were watching goldfish in a bowl. He was huge!

"Get back, girls," Madame Swann ordered, shooing them against the mirrored wall. "What does he want?" she muttered. "And why isn't the Fairy Queen coming to our rescue?"

"The Fairy Queen?" Megan whispered to Jessica. "How could she help?"

Jessica looked taken aback by the question. "With her magic, of course," she whispered. "But nobody has seen her recently. And strange things keep happening that she'd usually put right. The rumour is, that—"

Jessica broke off as the giant's massive fingers began fumbling to open the window, and the girls screamed even louder. "He's trying to get in," sobbed a girl whose hair was a pretty pale blue.

"Girls, we must leave immediately,"

Madame Swann shouted. "Follow me!"

Her class didn't need telling twice.
Screaming and crying, the girls rushed after
Madame Swann. But Megan had noticed
something. The giant seemed upset that
everyone was running away. His shoulders
had sagged and his mouth was turned
down. And was that really a tear in his eye?

Jessica was halfway out of the room
when Megan called her back. "Hold on,"
she said. "I don't think he means any
harm. He just looks sad."

Jessica stopped and stared at the giant.
"I don't know," she said hesitantly. "My
dad said he was dangerous. I really think
we should go with the others."

"Just give me a minute," Megan said,
then she turned and bravely addressed the
giant. "What… What are you doing here?

Are you all right? You look upset."

The giant shook his head, a tear spilling down his cheek. "I'm sorry about these here buildings," he said. "I didn't mean to break them. But this man, he came to the Misty Mountains and told me I had to come here to learn to dance. I said no, but he waved his wand and then my feet, they just came here themselves, like."

"I see," Megan replied politely, although she didn't really see at all. Her mind was racing. Was the man with the wand Sorcero? The Fairy Queen had guessed he'd be making trouble – but then maybe in the Land of Eight Kingdoms there were lots of men with wands…

"And it's terrible annoying but my feet, they just keep dancing, and…" He paused and Megan saw faint wisps of black and

purple smoke swirling round his toes. "Eh up. Here we go again."

In the next moment, the giant's feet were jerkily dancing on the pavement outside the ballet academy. The building shook, windows smashed and a silver lamp post fell over with a loud clang.

"Stop!" Megan cried in alarm. "Stop!"

"I can't!" the giant shouted. "That's the problem, see. I can't stop! Not till I've learned the dance of the Silver Snowflake!"

Megan bit her lip. The giant looked more like a snowplough than a snowflake. "What's the dance of the Silver Snowflake?" she asked Jessica. "Do you know it?"

"Well, yes, but—" Jessica began.

"Could you teach him?" Megan interrupted. "It might break the spell that he's under." She was sure this was Sorcero's doing now. The black and purple smoke round the giant's feet was just the same as she'd seen in her music-box mirror.

Jessica still looked nervous, but after a moment she gave a tiny nod. "All right," she said. "As long as you stay with me."

"Of course I will," Megan replied. "We're friends, aren't we?"

Jessica smiled. "OK, then."

Megan stepped towards the giant, who'd stopped dancing now and was leaning against a nearby building, panting and red in the face. "Excuse me, Mr Giant," she called. "What's your name?"

"Olaf," the giant wheezed.

"Well, Olaf, my friend Jessica will teach you the dance of the Silver Snowflake."

The giant bent down and beamed through the window. "Oh! That would be awful kind." And he gave a little jump for joy that cracked the studio windows.

Megan winced as a nearby building collapsed in a heap of bricks. If Olaf had a dancing lesson here in Silver City, the whole place would be ruined within minutes. "Let's go somewhere with more space to practise," she suggested.

"Maybe the Misty Mountains?"

Olaf beamed. "Good thinking," he said. "Stand back." Then he pushed through the broken window with his enormous fist.

Megan and Jessica clung to each other in fear as the window shattered and shards of glass flew everywhere, but then Olaf slipped his hand through the space, palm upwards, and they realized that he was offering them a ride.

Jessica still looked doubtful, so Megan grabbed her hand and squeezed it. "Come on," she said. "It'll be all right."

Together, they gingerly climbed on to Olaf's hand and he pulled them out of the building and popped them up on his shoulder. "All right!" he said, his voice sounding louder than ever now that they were so near his face. "Hang on to me ear

if things get bumpity. Next stop – the Misty Mountains."

He was about to stride away when a squeal of fright came up from one of the dancers below. "Hey! The giant's kidnapping the new girls. Call the guards!"

"He's not kidnapping us," Megan called down. "It's fine. He's really nice!"

Unfortunately, her voice was swallowed up by more screams, and then the sound of sirens.

"Oh no," Olaf wailed. "This all be going wrong now. Hold on, up there. I'm going to run, I am!"

As Olaf thundered off in a panic, Megan and Jessica were bounced up and down on his shoulder. Megan clutched his big hairy ear, and Jessica hung on to Megan for dear life. The ground seemed a terrifyingly long way down and Megan couldn't help wondering if she'd just made a dreadful mistake. What if this was all part of Sorcero's plan? What if the giant was going to take them straight to the evil enchanter's lair?

The Magic Secrets Box

Chapter Six

*I*t was too late to stop the giant now though, Megan thought desperately, as he ran through the streets, striding easily across buildings and roads. All she could do was hold on tight and just hope that her instincts about him being harmless had been right.

They reached the edge of the city, and Megan could see huge black mountains with fleecy mist drifting around their peaks. Ahead lay deep pine forests, twisting blue rivers and lakes, and open green fields.

Suddenly, Olaf stopped. "Uh-oh, the dancing's coming on again. Hold tight!"

And then he was jigging and twirling once more, black and purple smoke swirling about his feet as they kicked out helplessly. He swayed and swung, panting and breathless, sending Megan and Jessica crashing up and down on his shoulder. During one particularly vigorous spin they toppled right off their perch, tumbling down head first into the giant's shirt pocket.

"Mmmf," spluttered Megan, as she got a mouthful of pocket-fluff.

"Yuck," cried Jessica, fighting her way out of a giant-sized spotted handkerchief.

The girls scrambled up inside the pocket and peered out, just as Olaf's dancing slowed.

"Phew," he said, mopping his brow. "Now then, girlies," he went on, turning to peer down at his shoulder. "Oh no," he groaned when he saw that they were no longer there. "I ain't gone and lost them girlies, do I? My ma always did say I was the clumsiest, stupidest giant of—"

"We're here," Megan called, waving at

the giant from inside his pocket.

"My girlies!" he beamed. "Do I be glad to see you again. I thought I'd lost you. We're here at the foot of the Misty Mountains. Let me help you down."

He plucked the girls gently from his pocket and set them on the ground. Then he kicked a few fallen tree trunks out of the way, stamped the ground down flat, and clapped his hands. "Now then! How about this here dancing lesson, eh? Turn me into a dainty Silver Snowflake."

Jessica smiled up at him. "OK," she said. "Let's go through a few basic steps."

Jessica's dancing lesson began, and Megan learned the movements along with Olaf. Jessica was a good, patient teacher, and Olaf was surprisingly nimble on his feet. It wasn't long before all three of

them were twirling like snowflakes on their tiptoes, leaping gracefully through the air, and perfecting the tiny fluttering steps that Jessica showed them.

Megan had to hide a smile. Who would have thought that she'd be here in a magical land, learning the Silver Snowflake dance with an enormous giant? Jessica, too, seemed to be enjoying herself hugely. Gone was the unhappy face she'd worn when Megan first met her. Now she seemed confident and full of smiles.

"I think we're almost there," Jessica said after a while. "I reckon you could dance the whole routine now without making any mistakes and, fingers crossed, that might just break the spell."

Olaf gave a happy sigh. "Oh, I do be hoping so," he said. "I can teach all my friends to be snowflakes, too. We will be a giant blizzard, and that's the truth now."

"From the top, then," Jessica said. "A one-two-three…"

But before Jessica could go on, the sound of sirens burst into the air … in the distance at first, but growing louder by the second. They all turned to see a group of figures approaching. As they grew nearer, Megan could see they were guards riding flying horses. Madame Swann was with them.

"Girls, are you all right? Has he hurt you?" she cried, waving down at them.

"We're fine!" Jessica called back.

"Attention!" shouted one of the guards through a loudhailer. "You, the tall monstrous thing. Stop right there, and do not harm those girls! We have freeze-shooters and we will use them!"

"Freeze-shooters?" Megan mouthed to Jessica, not understanding.

She nodded, looking alarmed. "They freeze you to solid ice," she replied. "It takes two weeks to thaw out, apparently."

Olaf held up his hands. "Oh no, don't be freezing me," he pleaded. "I hates being cold, so I do. And—" Then an agonized look spread over his face. "Not now, you stupid feet," he hissed, as they began twitching. He let out a wail as black and

purple smoke appeared round his toes, and the spell worked its magic again, forcing him to dance.

The guards backed away, looking wary, and their horses reared up in fright. "Hey! Tall guy! We just told you to stop," the guard bellowed through his loudhailer. "If you don't stand still right now—"

"He can't," Megan yelled. "He's under a spell. If you wait, he'll stop in a minute."

The guards didn't seem convinced by Megan's explanation. "Causing a public disturbance," one said, consulting a well-thumbed rulebook. "Damage to public buildings. Er… Dancing when not supposed to. Let's freeze him anyway. He's a menace."

"Oh, please don't," Megan shouted desperately. "He's our friend!"

Thankfully, in the next moment, the black and purple smoke vanished and the giant's feet were still once more. "Ooer," he groaned, catching his breath. "Sorry about that. Me and my feet, we have different ideas about what we're doing. What were you fellas saying just now?"

"We were saying, we're arresting you," one of the guards declared, pointing what looked like a water-pistol at Olaf.

Megan guessed this was the freeze-shooter. "Please, no!" she cried, stepping in front of the giant. "Don't shoot!"

"I didn't be meaning no harm, see," Olaf said, looking bewildered. "I'm sorry about all them buildings I done broken. My brother's good at mending things, he'll—"

"Silence!" commanded the guard with the freeze-shooter. "I've heard enough. Prepare to be iced."

"Wait," came the crisp, bossy voice of Madame Swann. "Put that freeze-shooter down, young man. RIGHT NOW!"

The Magic Secrets Box

Chapter Seven

*E*veryone stared as Madame Swann guided her horse down to the ground, dismounted and walked around thoughtfully. Then she beamed. "This is perfect," she said. "Absolutely perfect. This circle of flattened ground in the centre, these tree-trunk seats round the edge – this is the ideal outdoor theatre."

"So … the ballet company could hold their performance after all," Megan realized with a smile. "Right here!"

"Indeed," said Madame Swann. She smiled up at Olaf. "You are a genius,"

she told him. "I would like to shake your
hand, but unfortunately I can't reach. And
you two," she went on, turning to Jessica
and Megan, "have saved the day by
helping our giant friend. We must tell
everyone that the concert is on again and
inform the King and Queen immediately."
Then she fixed the guards with a frosty
stare. "And if you so much as freeze a
single hair on this giant's head, you will
have me to deal with. Understand?"

The guard with the freeze-shooter
lowered it meekly. "Yes, Madame Swann."

"Very well. You are dismissed," she told
the guards, with a wave of her hand. "And
now – we must prepare for our show!"

Olaf gave a small cough as the guards
flew away. "Just one thing, your ladyship
… highness … er … teacher-ness," he said

nervously. "I need to do a quick Silver
Snowflake dance, to break the
enchantment on me feet, like. May I?"

Megan and Jessica explained the
situation, and Madame Swann listened
gravely. "It would be my pleasure to
dance it with you," she said, taking off her
cloak and dropping a curtsey before
Olaf's hairy foot.

"Let's *all* dance it," Megan suggested.
"Ready? A-one-two-three…"

And the four of them performed the
Silver Snowflake dance together,
spinning, twirling and fluttering just like
real snowflakes. As Olaf danced, black
and purple smoke trailed out of his toes,
becoming fainter and fainter, and then
finally stopping. The enchantment had
been broken!

At the end of the dance, all four of
them cheered – even Madame Swann,
who hadn't struck Megan as the cheering
kind. "Marvellous," Madame Swann said,
clapping her hands at the giant. "You
must come to the performance. Bring a
friend or two. You'll be our guests of
honour."

Olaf blushed. "That do be kind," he

said gruffly. "But first I got a little favour to ask me brother. Some buildings to mend. We'll do 'em up ever so nice, that we will." He waved cheerfully. "See you later!"

He strode off towards the mountains, and Madame Swann called the flying horse over. "We can all return to Silver City on my steed," she said, helping Jessica and Megan up on to the horse's glossy white back, before elegantly leaping on herself.

The horse neighed and shook out its huge white feathery wings and then, with a single gallop, they were up in the air, soaring above the Eight Kingdoms. "That's the kingdom of the Emerald Seas in the distance, look," Jessica said, pointing it out. "And there on the right you can just see the edge of the Evergreen Woods."

The Magic Secrets Box

"It's beautiful here," Megan said, her eyes shining as she took in the amazing view. Home seemed a long way away.

When Madame Swann's horse landed outside the ballet academy, a great cheer went up from the other girls, who rushed outside to greet Megan and Jessica. "You were so brave," the girl with blue hair said admiringly.

"You should have seen Jessica teaching the giant to dance," Megan said, feeling pleased that her new friend was the centre of attention now. "She was awesome."

"And thanks to these two, our show is back on tonight," Madame Swann said. She put her hands on her hips in mock-stern fashion, although her eyes were twinkling. "So what are you all doing here? We must get practising immediately!"

Megan didn't think she'd ever felt happier as the ballet show ended that evening. It had been an enormous success. The King and Queen of Silver City had come to the performance and clapped harder than anybody. The White Witches of the Evergreen Forest had also flown in for the occasion, and cast some firework spells at the end, making the darkening sky crackle with colour and light. And Olaf the dancing giant had come along with his brother, and their applause had been so loud it sounded like thunder. They'd repaired all the damage in Silver City and now that the spell had been broken, no giant would cause trouble there again.

"Although we're thinking of setting up

our own dance troupe thingy," Olaf told
Madame Swann. "So if there's any chance
you might pop over for a visit sometime
and give us a lesson or two…"

"Any time," she promised.

Best of all, Jessica seemed to be getting
on really well with the other girls now,
Megan noticed. Teaching a giant to dance
had obviously given her a giant-sized
helping of confidence.

Just then, Megan heard the tinkling
melody from her musical box, and
everything started to blur and sway before
her eyes. Oh no. What was happening?
She had the feeling her adventure may be
coming to an end – but had she done
enough to help free the Fairy Queen?

The Magic Secrets Box

Chapter Eight

She ran to find Jessica and hugged her quickly. "I've got to go," she said. "But I so enjoyed meeting you. I'll never forget our adventure together!"

Jessica looked confused. "You're going already? But you'll be back at ballet class tomorrow, right?"

Megan shook her head. "I don't think so," she said. "I can't explain. I don't belong here and I must return home. That's all I can tell you."

Jessica smiled. "Thank you for being my friend," she said quietly.

And with that, the tinkling music grew
louder in Megan's ears, and everything
vanished.

Once again, Megan felt herself being
pulled very fast through the air, with
images of Jessica and Olaf and Madame
Swann whirling before her eyes. Then her
feet touched the ground, and she blinked.
She was back in her bedroom, and
wearing her normal clothes again. She
glanced up at the clock to see that no
time had passed at all.

"Well done," came a silvery voice above
the sound of the tinkling music. Megan
looked down to see the figure of the Fairy
Queen smiling up at her from the music
box. "I gather you were successful."

Megan frowned, not understanding. She still felt rather dazed after all that had happened. Then she noticed that there was a pretty pink ribbon coiled up in her music box – just like the ribbons on the ballet shoes she'd been wearing. She smiled – how lovely to have a souvenir from her magical adventure! But then her face fell as she realized that the Fairy Queen was still trapped in the box. "It didn't work," she said. "You're not free."

"No," said the Fairy Queen. "I'm not free, but already I can feel that Sorcero's spell is weakening – look, I can move my head a little. I couldn't do that before."

Megan watched as the Fairy Queen tilted her head from side to side, smiling in delight. "Tell me everything," the Fairy Queen begged. "While I am a prisoner in your world, I need you to be my eyes and ears in the Eight Kingdoms. Was all well? Did the people seem happy there?"

Megan told the Fairy Queen about her adventure – how she'd befriended Jessica, and how they'd met the giant and helped him break the enchantment. "The spell wasn't just to make him dance, it was to make him dance in Silver City," Megan explained. "Whoever cast the spell must have known he'd do a lot of damage."

"That sounds like Sorcero," the Fairy Queen murmured in dismay.

Megan nodded. "There was black and purple smoke round the giant's feet whenever the enchantment took hold," she said. "Just like the smoke I saw him use when he took your magic."

The Fairy Queen nodded. "It is as I thought," she said. "Sorcero is out to cause trouble. I'm sure he was intending to return to Silver City later on and banish the giant with another spell, thus fooling everyone into thinking that he was a hero." Then she smiled. "Still, by helping Jessica – and Olaf – you managed to spoil his plan and lessen the enchantment on me. You have proved that you are the perfect person to help break the spell completely – if you want to go on helping me, that is?"

"Yes, please!" Megan breathed. "I'd love to. I'm so glad I saw you in the shop this morning."

"Megan!" came a shout from downstairs. "Lunch is ready!"

Megan jumped to her feet. "I'll be back as soon as I can," she said. Then she noticed that the music seemed to be dying away, and the colour was fading from the Fairy Queen's face. "Oh no, don't go," she cried. "What's happening?"

"Until next time," the Fairy Queen murmured … and a heartbeat later, the music had stopped and the Fairy Queen was still and stiff again.

Megan touched the end of her wand, but it just felt hard and cold now. She closed the lid, placed the music box carefully on her dressing table, and

dropped into a graceful curtsey in front of it. Madame Swann would have been proud of her, she thought with a smile. "Until next time," she repeated in a whisper.

Then she went down for lunch, hugging the secrets of her magical music box to herself. What adventure would she have next in the Land of Eight Kingdoms? She couldn't wait to find out.

Take a peak at Megan's next adventure,
The Great Mermaid Rescue
– out now!

…Megan's feet had vanished and in their place was a gleaming blue fish-tail. She'd been magically transformed into a mermaid, with a sparkly green top and a pink shell necklace!

"Whoa," she laughed, flicking her tailfin and sending herself skimming through the water at top speed. Being a mermaid was awesome, she thought joyfully, as a shoal of small red fish bustled past. Her hair streamed out behind her as she swam, the water cool and clear against her skin.

Then she heard voices and stopped to listen. They were too far away to make out, but Megan remembered how befriending a girl in the Silver City had weakened Sorcero's spell on the Fairy Queen. She was determined to make a friend in the Emerald Seas, too, so she decided to investigate.

She flicked her tail again and went whizzing along the seabed, passing green waving fronds of seaweed, an enormous scuttling crab and colourful sea urchins. Tiny blue fish darted in and out of rocks as if they were playing tag, and a large flat ray rose majestically through the water further ahead.

Megan slowed down as the voices became louder. She could now see a group of other mermaids in the distance, perched on a large circle of white rocks on the seabed, deep in conversation. Megan ducked behind a rock, suddenly feeling shy.

The mermaids wore sparkly tops like

Megan, and had hair in pastel shades of blue, green, pink and lavender. They were all listening to one mermaid in particular, who was sitting in the middle. She had long lilac hair and a glittery silver bikini top and was leaning forward talking excitedly.

"You should've seen the sea monster," the mermaid said. "It looked soooo ferocious. It had massive teeth this big," she went on, waving her arms dramatically to demonstrate, "and fins so huge they could knock a whale off course. It's true!"

Megan felt a shiver run down her spine as she listened to the lilac-haired mermaid's words. *Is this something to do with Sorcero?* she wondered fearfully. The sooner she could return to the safety of her bedroom the better!